Lucy's Amazing Friend

by Stephanie Workman

illustrated by Tim Raynes

PISCATAQUA PRESS

Lucy's Amazing Friend

Published by Piscataqua Press
An imprint of RiverRun Bookstore
142 Fleet St.
Portsmouth, NH 03801

www.piscataquapress.com
www.riverrunbookstore.com

Printed in the United States of America

ISBN: 978-1-939739-39-1

For my husband Tim
and
The Walker Family

To the Amazing Boyce Family
Stephanie Workman
2014

  Today at recess eight-year-old Lucy noticed a new kid drawing by himself. Curious, she walked over to him.

  "Hi, I'm Lucy," she said with a smile on her face. The boy ignored her and continued to draw.

  Lucy looked down at his drawing and noticed how awesome it was.

  "I really like your picture," she said. The boy still paid no attention.

  Confused, Lucy walked away.

When it was time to go inside Lucy marched right over to Miss Miller's desk.

"Yes, Lucy?" asked Miss Miller.

"Why doesn't the new boy in Miss Reed's class like me? I said hi and he ignored me," she said.

"Lucy, that's Daniel. He has autism," Miss Miller responded.

"What's autism?" asked Lucy.

"People living with autism sometimes have a hard time speaking and understanding things that come easy to us," said Miss Miller. "Their brains work differently. They feel things differently, and sometimes they have trouble making eye contact. That doesn't mean you should stop saying hi to him, though."

The next day at recess Lucy walked over to Daniel who was sitting with a woman this time.

"Hi, I'm Lucy," she said.

"Hi, Lucy, I'm Ellen and this is Daniel," the woman replied.

Daniel didn't look over.

"Are you his babysitter?" Lucy asked.

"No, I'm his aide," said Ellen. "I help Daniel with his lessons and staying on a schedule that helps him throughout the day. Today he was late for school so it's been a hard day for him. Maybe he'll want to play tomorrow."

Lucy went over to her friends Sophia and Flynn. They immediately asked her why she was talking to Daniel.

"I wanted him to play with us," replied Lucy.

"He's weird," said Flynn.

"Yeah, I saw him kicking and screaming on my way to the bathroom this morning," said Sophia.

Sophia and Flynn both giggled. Lucy didn't care. She wanted to be Daniel's friend.

The next morning it was raining, but by recess time it had stopped. As the kids played outside, Daniel walked over to the corner of the roof and stood underneath the falling water. The other kids began to point and laugh at him.

This bothered Lucy. She walked over to Daniel and stood underneath the falling water too. As they stood side by side getting wet, Daniel looked at her for the first time up close.

From then on Lucy and Daniel played together at recess. Some days they drew in silence, other days they played on the swings. Daniel liked to swing around in circles while Lucy swung as high as she could go.

On the days Lucy joined the other kids to play tag, Daniel watched on the sidelines.

Whenever the bell rang Daniel covered his ears. Loud noises
bothered him.

When the lights inside were too bright, he'd put on his sunglasses.

Not only did Daniel love drawing, water, and the swings, he also loved music and movies. So did Lucy.

One day Daniel's mom invited Lucy over to play. They spent the whole time in Daniel's room listening to their favorite song. They must have listened to it twenty times.

When Daniel did speak, it turned out that he had an incredible memory. He could recite every line from all of his favorite movies, all of the actors and actresses in the movie, the year the movie was made, and any awards it won, along with any interesting facts about the movie.

Daniel was unlike any kid Lucy had ever met. He was amazing!
She wished the other kids could see that too.

Lucy's birthday was coming up and she decided to have her party at a water park. Everyone from her class was invited and Daniel was too. When the other kids found out Daniel was invited, they weren't too happy. Lucy didn't care.

At Lucy's party Daniel sat with his mother and watched the kids go up and down the water slides all afternoon. None of the kids paid any attention to him except Lucy.

"Daniel, don't you want to go down the water slides?" Lucy asked.
 Daniel shook his head no.
 "I'll go down the slide with you," she said.
 "Come on, Daniel," said his mom. "I know when we get home you'll
be upset if you don't go down once."

Hesitantly, Daniel stood up and followed Lucy to one of the slides. When they reached the top Flynn and Sophia got in line behind them. They were surprised to see Daniel.

When it was Lucy and Daniel's turn, Daniel froze, scared to go down.

"You can do it, Daniel," said Lucy. "I promise I'll be with you the whole time."

"You can do it, Daniel!" the other kids joined in.

Daniel took a deep breath and sat down on the mat behind Lucy. She looked back at him and smiled.

"One, two, three!" the kids yelled.

On the count of three, Lucy and Daniel pushed their mat down the slide. Faster and faster they went. As Lucy shrieked with laughter, Daniel shrieked along. A face which usually remained blank was filled with the biggest smile you can imagine.

After they splashed into the water and came up again, Daniel shouted, "Again!"

The rest of the day Lucy, Daniel, and the other kids went down the slides. Daniel went down with everyone.

They all had a blast together. Daniel liked having fun just like they did. He wasn't so weird after all.

The following Monday at recess Daniel sat alone on the steps. Before Lucy had a chance to go over to him Sophia and Flynn beat her to it. This made her happy.

"Would you like to go on the swings with us?" Sophia asked Daniel.

Daniel nodded yes. He stood up and followed them to the swings where Lucy was waiting for them, already swinging away.

Sophia and Flynn thought Lucy was right: Daniel WAS amazing!